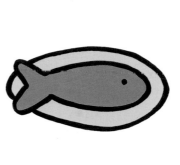

A Cheshire Studio Book

NORTH-SOUTH BOOKS

New York · London

Florence Page Jaques

There Once Was a Puffin

Illustrated by Shari Halpern

Oh, there once was a Puffin
Just the shape of a muffin,

And he lived on an island
In the
bright
blue
sea!

He ate little fishes
That were most delicious,

And he had them for supper
And he
had
them
for tea.

But this poor little Puffin,

He couldn't play nothin'

For he hadn't anybody
To
      play
         with
            at all.

So he sat on his island,
And he cried for a while, and
He felt very lonely,
And he
    felt
        very
            small.

Then along came the fishes,
And they said, "If you wishes,
You can have us for playmates,
Instead
of
for
tea!"

So they now play together

In all sorts of weather,

And the Puffin eats pancakes,
Like you
and
like
me.

**To Ali, oh Ali,
bird expert, fish expert, and pancake expert,
and special thanks to Joe —S.H.**

A CHESHIRE STUDIO BOOK
Published in the United States by North-South Books Inc., New York.
Published simultaneously in Great Britain, Canada, Australia, and
New Zealand in 2003 by North-South Books, an imprint
of Nord-Süd Verlag AG, Gossau Zürich, Switzerland.

Library of Congress Cataloging-in-Publication Data is available.
A CIP catalogue record for this book is available from The British Library.

ISBN 0-7358-1770-7 (trade edition)
1 3 5 7 9 HC 10 8 6 4 2
ISBN 0-7358-1771-5 (library edition)
1 3 5 7 9 LE 10 8 6 4 2
Printed in Hong Kong

For more information about our books, and the authors and artists
who create them, visit our web site: www.northsouth.com